LITTLE SIMON

An imprint of Simon & Schuster Children's Publishing Division • 1230 Avenue of the Americas, New York, New York 10020 • First Little Simon paperback edition October 2019 • Copyright © 2019 by Simon & Schuster, Inc. All rights reserved, including the right of reproduction in whole or in part in any form. LITTLE SIMON is a registered trademark of Simon & Schuster, Inc., and associated colophon is a trademark of Simon & Schuster, Inc. For information about special discounts for bulk purchases, please contact Simon & Schuster Special Sales at 1-866-506-1949 or business@simonandschuster.com. The Simon & Schuster Speakers Bureau can bring authors to your live event. For more information or to book an event contact the Simon & Schuster Speakers Bureau at 1-866-248-3049 or visit our website at www.simonspeakers.com.

Series designed by Laura Roode. The text of this book was set in Usherwood. Manufactured in the United States of America 0919 MTN   10 9 8 7 6 5 4 3 2 1

Cataloging-in-Publication Data is available for this title from the Library of Congress.

ISBN 978-1-5344-4949-7 (hc)
ISBN 978-1-5344-4948-0 (pbk)
ISBN 978-1-5344-4950-3 (eBook)

the adventures of
SOPHIE MOUSE

15

The Missing Tooth Fairy

By Poppy Green • Illustrated by Jennifer A. Bell

LITTLE SIMON

New York London Toronto Sydney New Delhi

Contents

chapter 1

A Bite of a Biscuit

Sophie Mouse rolled over in bed and opened her eyes. The first thing she saw was her newest acorn, sitting on her bedside table.

Sophie smiled. The acorn was smooth, shiny, and orange-red. She had found it the day before.

Sophie got up and peered underneath her bed. She pulled out a box.

It held her acorn collection. There were brown ones and green ones.

There were round ones and pointy ones. Some had acorn caps and some did not. No two were exactly alike. Sophie placed her new acorn inside the box.

But then Sophie had a thought. No, a vision: all of her acorns, lined up neatly on a shelf. An acorn display!

As an artist, Sophie loved the idea.

Sophie looked at the shelves on her wall. The lowest one was cluttered with paint tins, library books, and papers.

Sophie went to work. She cleaned out the empty paint tins. She organized the rest in her art box. She put the library books in her backpack so she'd remember to return them. She sorted papers.

Soon Sophie had a clean, empty shelf. A blank canvas! Onto it, she emptied her acorn collection.

Sophie arranged and rearranged. First by color, then by size. Then she tried mixing the acorns up a bit. Yes, she liked that arrangement best.

Now Sophie could look at her acorns all the time!

"Sophie!" Mrs. Mouse called from downstairs. "Breakfast!"

"Okay!" Sophie called.

She took one last look at her acorn display and smiled. Then she ran downstairs. Her little brother, Winston, was already at the table.

Sophie's whiskers twitched. "Something smells yummy!" Sophie exclaimed.

Mrs. Mouse was pulling a baking sheet out of the oven. "I'm trying a new biscuit recipe," she explained. "Will you and Winston tell me what you think?"

Sophie and Winston nodded excitedly. Their mom was the best baker in Pine Needle Grove. Muffins, pies, cakes, breads—Lily Mouse made them all at her bakery in town. But first, they had to pass the taste test at home.

Mrs. Mouse put a plate of biscuits on the table. "I may have overcooked them a bit," she warned them. "Try to imagine they're softer."

Sophie reached for a biscuit. Before she tasted it, her nose picked

up a scent. Some kind of berry. Sophie took a bite. Oh, it *was* a little hard. But so good! Buttery and with a mild, nutty flavor.

"I taste raspberry!" said Winston.

"And oats?" Sophie added.

Mrs. Mouse laughed. "Impressive!" she cried. "Yes! They are raspberry-oat biscuits!"

Sophie took another big bite.

Ow!

This time she felt a weird pain in her mouth. Sophie spit out the biscuit.

Lily Mouse frowned. "Oh no," she said. "Is it that bad?"

Sophie shook her head. The biscuits were delicious. Sophie wanted to tell her mom so. But first she had to see what was going on in her mouth.

Sophie got up and ran to the bathroom. She leaned close to the mirror and opened her mouth.

Sophie's top front tooth was crooked.
She touched it gently. The tooth *moved*!
Sophie could wiggle it back and forth.

Oh no! Sophie thought. *My tooth is loose!*

chapter 2

Too Much Tooth Talk

Sophie slowly walked back into the kitchen. Her whiskers were standing on end and her eyes were wide in alarm.

Lily Mouse could see something was wrong. "What's the matter?" she asked.

Sophie didn't answer. She was afraid to speak.

"Sophie, dear," Mrs. Mouse said.
Now she looked very worried. "Are
you okay?"

Slowly Sophie opened her mouth.
She pointed to the loose tooth.

Mrs. Mouse breathed a sigh of relief. "Oh Sophie! Your first loose tooth!"

She smiled and gave Sophie a hug. "That's so exciting!"

Sophie closed her mouth. Exciting? Try terrifying! Her tooth was *moving*.

And sooner or later . . . it was going to *fall out*!

"Can I see?" Winston asked eagerly. He leaned in close, waiting for Sophie to open up. She pursed her lips tightly and shook her head.

"It's okay to talk," Mrs. Mouse assured her. "Your tooth won't fall out until it's good and ready."

Sophie didn't want to risk it.

So she didn't eat her breakfast.

While getting dressed, she pulled her jumper on over her head very carefully.

And Sophie didn't say a word all morning—even as she and Winston walked to school.

So Winston filled the silence. "I heard that sharks lose teeth every week," he said.

Ugh. That sounded awful to Sophie. She wished Winston would talk about something else. Anything other than teeth. But since Sophie wasn't talking, she couldn't tell him that.

"I can't wait for *my* teeth to get wiggly!" Winston went on. He looked up at Sophie. "What does it feel like? Can you make it move with your tongue?"

Sophie gasped. Could she? She hadn't tried that. Did she want to know? Oh, why wouldn't Winston talk about something else?

"I've never seen a tooth *outside* of someone's mouth," Winston said. "I wonder what it will look like when it falls out."

Sophie stopped. Winston walked on, then noticed Sophie wasn't there. He looked back at her.

Sophie pointed at Winston. Then she made a motion like she was zipping her mouth shut. And turning the key. She gave him a pleading look and clasped her hands together.

The message was clear: *You. Be quiet. Please.*

Winston got it. "Okay, okay," he said. He didn't say another word all the way to school.

chapter 3

Too Good to Be True?

Inside the one-room schoolhouse, Mrs. Wise was taking attendance. Sophie and Winston slipped into their seats just in time.

Sophie looked over at her friends, Hattie Frog and Owen Snake. She gave them a wave. Sophie was glad that now she *had* to be quiet. Mrs. Wise was about to start the math lesson.

But Sophie couldn't concentrate.
She was so distracted by her tooth.
A couple of times, Sophie dared to
feel the tooth with her tongue.

The first time, it didn't move.

The second time, Sophie was feeling braver. She pushed at the tooth a little harder. It definitely moved!

Startled, Sophie jumped a little bit in her seat.

Mrs. Wise saw it. "What is it, Sophie?" Mrs. Wise asked. "Is something the matter?"

Uh-oh. Sophie didn't know what to do. She shook her head no. She hoped that would be enough of an answer for the teacher.

It wasn't. Mrs. Wise was waiting for an explanation. Sophie had to say something.

She opened her mouth. She spoke slowly and carefully. "I . . . have . . . a . . . loose . . . tooth," she said.

Sophie felt everyone looking at her.

Then Mrs. Wise smiled and said, "Ah! I see." She turned back to the chalkboard. The students did too. The math lesson went on as if nothing had happened.

But at recess Hattie and Owen came rushing up to Sophie. "So?" said Owen.

"Let's see," said Hattie.

Sophie sighed. She showed them
which tooth it was.

"You don't seem too happy about it," Hattie pointed out gently. Sophie shrugged. Hattie knew her so well.

"It's going to fall out," Sophie said softly and carefully.

Owen looked confused. "Don't you want it to fall out?" he asked.

Sophie thought about it. "I do," she said. "I'm just . . . scared."

Hattie put an arm around Sophie's shoulders. She gave her friend a squeeze.

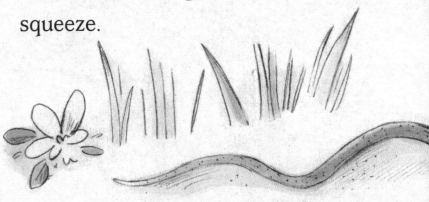

Ben Rabbit ran by. He skidded to a stop next to Sophie.

"I've lost two teeth," Ben told her. "Actually, I hopped off a swing and knocked them out."

Sophie winced. That sounded terrible!

"It's okay! They grew back!" Ben said. "See?" He smiled a huge, perfect smile. "And the best part was the tooth fairy came!"

"The tooth fairy?" Sophie said, confused.

Ben looked at her in disbelief. "You've never heard of the tooth fairy?" he asked. "When you lose a tooth, you put it under your pillow. While you sleep, the tooth fairy comes, takes your tooth, and leaves you something special."

Owen's eyes lit up. "What did you get?" he asked Ben.

"A four-leaf clover!" Ben replied.

Sophie let her mind wander away from her loose tooth. She let herself imagine.

If there really were a tooth fairy . . .

Sophie wasn't convinced that there was. It sounded too magical and wonderful to be true.

But if there were . . . what would it leave for her?

chapter 4

A Week of Worries

All week Sophie was very careful about her tooth.

She was careful about what she ate. She wanted only soft foods. Her mom made her some homemade applesauce. Her dad packed different soups for lunch each day: carrot chowder, cream of broccoli, and mushroom bisque. Sophie tore her bread and muffins into tiny pieces. That way, she didn't need to bite into them.

Sophie was careful when she brushed her teeth. She brushed everywhere *except* the loose tooth. *Do I really need to clean it?* Sophie asked herself. *It's going to fall out anyway.*

Sophie was even careful when she played. On Wednesday afternoon, she went to Forget-Me-Not Lake with Hattie and Owen. Hattie hopped from rock to rock. Sophie made a move to follow her. But she stopped herself. What if she fell and knocked her tooth out?

At school Sophie stayed off the swings and the monkey bars. Instead she picked violets along the edge of the playground. She figured she could use them to make a purple paint that she loved.

Careful as she was, Sophie's tooth got looser each day. She didn't like seeing it in the mirror. It was so crooked now that it was leaning into the tooth next to it.

On Sunday, Sophie and Winston

went to Piper's birthday party. For a little while Sophie forgot about her tooth. She joined in the scavenger hunt. She was excited for Piper as she opened her gifts.

Then it was time for birthday cake! They all sang "Happy Birthday" to Piper. She blew out the candles and cut the cake.

Sophie's heart sank. It was seed cake, filled with pumpkin and sun-flower seeds, plus caramel and nou-gat. It looked delicious. But it also looked sticky and dense.

Piper's dad offered her a piece.

"No thank you," Sophie said.

Back at home Sophie complained to her parents. "This loose tooth!" she cried. "It's really messing up my week!"

"I'm sorry," Lily Mouse said sympathetically. "How about I make you a sweet treat that you *can* eat?"

Sophie's mom whipped
up a bowl of smooth,
creamy chocolate pudding.
She served it to Sophie in a fancy dish.

"Thanks, Mom," Sophie said.

She scooped up a large spoonful
and put it in her mouth. Mmmmm.

It was chocolaty and sweet. And so cold. Sophie could feel the cold pudding on her gums.

Especially right in front. Up top. Where her loose tooth was.

Sophie froze.

She felt around that area with her
tongue. It wasn't there! The tooth was
gone!

chapter 5

Lost . . .
and Found!

Where is the tooth? Sophie wondered, feeling panicked.

Her mouth was still full of pudding. Should she spit it out? What if the tooth was in there too? Or . . .

Sophie looked down.

There! The tooth was in the dish of pudding, right on top. *It must have fallen out when I took the bite!*

Sophie carefully picked out the tooth and rinsed it at the sink. "Mom! Dad! Winston!" Sophie cried. "My tooth fell out!"

They all hurried to Sophie's side.

"Let me see!" said Winston.

Sophie showed him the tooth in her hand. Then she smiled a big smile.

"Yep!" Winston said with a giggle. "There's a big space where it used to be."

Sophie ran into the bathroom. She looked in the mirror and laughed. Winston was right. There was a big space—a hole in her smile. It looked funny. But Sophie didn't care. The tooth was out! And she didn't even feel it happen.

Sophie ran upstairs to her room. She picked up her pillow and placed the

tooth underneath—just like Ben said.
Just in case there was a tooth fairy.

Except there probably wasn't. But
maybe there was.

Then Sophie remembered something else Ben had said.

"While you sleep, the tooth fairy

comes, takes your tooth, and leaves you something special."

Sophie frowned. If the tooth fairy took her tooth, she couldn't show it to her friends. Wouldn't Hattie and Owen want to see it?

The next morning Sophie got to school early. Mrs. Wise was still unpacking her tote bag. Hattie and Owen were near the coat hooks.

Sophie snuck up behind Hattie. She tapped her on the shoulder. Hattie turned around. Sophie smiled

a huge smile. She poked her tongue into the empty space where her tooth used to be.

Hattie's eyes went wide. "Your tooth is gone!" she cried.

Sophie laughed. "Yep!" she replied. "It fell out yesterday!" Sophie reached into her backpack. She pulled out a small box that looked like a tiny treasure chest. She opened the lid. Inside was her tooth on a square of purple fabric.

Hattie and Owen leaned in close to see.

Hattie had a funny look on her face, like she wasn't sure what to think. "That used to be a part of your body," she said. "And now it's not."

Was it just Sophie's imagination? Or did Hattie sound a little grossed out?

"Wait," said Owen. "It fell out yesterday? But then why do you still have it?" He seemed disappointed. "I guess maybe there's no tooth fairy after all."

Sophie explained. "I didn't put it under my pillow." At this, Owen looked surprised. So Sophie went on. "I wanted to show it to you first. But I'll try it tonight."

Owen frowned. "On the second night?" he said. "Will that work?"

Sophie shrugged. "Why wouldn't it?" she replied confidently. But at the same time she felt a pang of regret. Had she made a mistake?

chapter 6

Fairy Ready!

Sophie got ready for bed early that night. By eight o'clock she had her pajamas on. She had brushed her teeth. She'd said good night to everyone.

And she had tucked her tooth underneath her pillow. Sophie decided to leave it inside the box. On its own the tooth was so small. She didn't want it to get lost.

Sophie tried reading in bed for a while, hoping to get sleepy. But she was too excited. It was hard to concentrate on her book.

She looked around her room. *What would the tooth fairy think of it?* Sophie wondered. *If there is a tooth fairy, of course.*

Right now the room was actually kind of messy.

Sophie hopped out of bed. It wasn't every night that a *fairy* might come visiting. She wanted to make a good impression.

So Sophie picked up her clothes from the floor and put them in her laundry basket. She put away the books that were under her bed. She tidied up her easel. She dusted off her nightstand. She found a few of Winston's toys and returned them to his room.

"That's better," Sophie said.

Sophie selected two of her newest paintings. She put them on display on her easel.

As she climbed back into bed, she straightened the acorns in her acorn collection.

Then, before she turned off the light, Sophie reached for the window. She propped it open, even though it was a breezy night. Ben hadn't said anything about needing to do that.

But otherwise, how would the tooth fairy get in? Sophie didn't want to leave anything to chance.

Sophie plumped up her pillow. She flicked the light off. She snuggled under her covers.

And she waited for sleep to come.

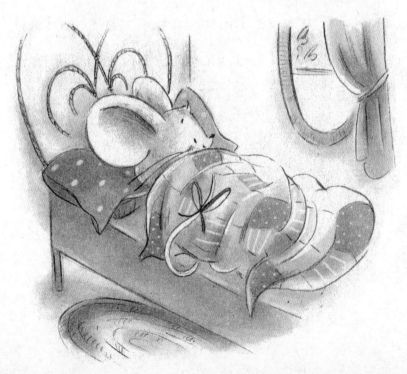

The next thing Sophie knew, a cho-
rus of very loud birds was singing a
morning song. Very, *very* loud birds.

Sophie rolled over and groaned.
Why were they so loud this morning? And why was it so cold? Sophie
felt a breeze blow across her ears.
She pulled her covers up over her
head.

Then suddenly
Sophie sat up. Now
she remembered!
She had left the
window open. And
she had left the
window open because . . .
Sophie looked under her pillow.

The box was still there. She peeked inside. The tooth was there too.

Sophie looked around the room. Everything was as it had been the night before. Nothing had moved. Nothing had changed. Nothing special had been left behind.

There was no sign anyone had
been there at all.

chapter 7

Teamwork!

"What if I missed my chance?" Sophie groaned.

She was sitting with Ben, Hattie, and Owen during art time. Mrs. Wise had passed out paper and colored pencils. They could draw on the theme of seasons. Or they could free draw.

"Maybe tooth fairies only come on

the first night," Sophie went on. "Oh, why did I wait to put the tooth under my pillow?"

Ben looked up from his autumn foliage drawing. "The tooth fairy will come," he told Sophie. "I just know it."

Hattie was coloring in the buds on a flowering tree. "Maybe he or she couldn't find your house," Hattie suggested.

Sophie thought about that. "How does the tooth fairy know where I live, anyway?" Sophie pondered.

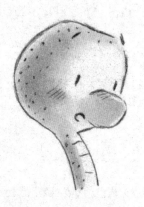

Owen shrugged. "We are talking about a fairy," he said. "There is a lot that is hard to explain."

Sophie's paper was still blank. She couldn't decide what to draw. In fact, she didn't feel like drawing. She felt like figuring out the mystery of the missing tooth fairy.

Could Hattie be right? What if the tooth fairy needed help finding her house? *How can I make it easier to find?* Sophie wondered.

Suddenly she had an idea.

Sophie grabbed a colored pencil and began to draw. In the center of her paper, she drew an oak tree. She labeled it SOPHIE'S HOUSE.

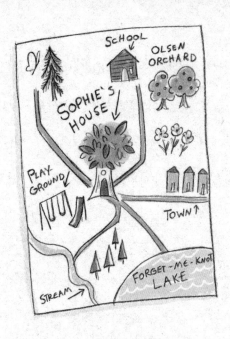

Then, around the oak tree, she drew symbols for other locations in Pine Needle Grove. She added symbols for the shops in town. She drew in the stream and the playground. She marked the locations of Olsen Orchard and Buttercup Patch.

Hattie leaned over to look at Sophie's paper. "What's that?" Hattie asked.

"A map," Sophie explained. "Maybe you're right. Maybe the tooth fairy just needs help finding my house."

Hattie's eyes lit up. "Great idea!" she exclaimed. "I'll make one too." Hattie put her springtime drawing aside. She got a clean sheet of paper. "Where can we leave them so the tooth fairy might find them?"

Owen took a new sheet of paper too.

"Let's make lots of copies," Owen suggested. "We'll put them up all over town!"

Ben joined in. All four of them made maps until art time was over. By then, they had about a dozen copies. Hattie even decorated each one with glitter glue—a *lot* of glitter glue.

"It will grab the fairy's attention," Hattie explained. She held up a glittery map. "Don't you think?"

Sophie laughed.

At the front of the classroom, Mrs. Wise flapped her wings. "Okay, class," she called out. "Art time is over. Please clean up."

Sophie collected all the finished maps.

"Meet outside after school?" Owen suggested. "We'll help you hang these up."

Ben and Hattie nodded in agreement.

Sophie beamed. She was grateful to have the help of her friends.

— chapter 8 —

Right This way

The four friends broke up into two teams. Sophie and Hattie both lived near the stream. Owen and Ben lived on the other side of town.

So Owen and Ben took half the maps. And Sophie and Hattie took the other half.

"We'll hang some on our way through town," Owen said. "One by the

library, one by Little Leaf Bookstore, and one by the General Store."

"And maybe one out by Goldmoss Pond," Ben added.

Sophie nodded. "And we'll cover our side of Pine Needle Grove," she said. "Thanks for your help!"

The teams parted ways. Owen and Ben took the path toward town. Sophie and Hattie went the other way through the tunnel of honeysuckle branches.

Sophie stopped at the first big tree they came to. It was a beautiful fir tree with long, drooping branches.

"How about one on here?"

Hattie nodded. "Let me give you a boost," she suggested. "After all, fairies fly. So the higher the map is, the better."

"Good thinking!" Sophie said.

Hattie crouched down in leapfrog position. Sophie climbed up and balanced on Hattie's back. Then Sophie reached up as high as she could. She found a spot where the tree's trunk was sticky with sap. Sophie pressed the glittery map right on that spot. It stuck like glue.

"Perfect!" Sophie declared.

Moving on, they hung a map on the main path to Butterfly Brook. They hung another on the side of Birch Tree Slide. They hung a couple down by the stream. And they hung their last map on the path to Forget-Me-Not Lake.

Then they headed for home. They got to Hattie's house first. Sophie thanked her for her help.

"You're welcome," Hattie replied.
"I bet the tooth fairy will be able to
find your house tonight."

Sophie nodded as she waved good-
bye. She hoped Hattie was right. They

had made a lot of maps. They had hung them all over. And they were certainly very eye-catching. Surely the tooth fairy would see *one* of the maps.

Right?

As she walked up to her front door, Sophie had one more idea.

She looked around on the forest floor. She gathered some of the longest twigs she could find and dragged them toward the front door. She arranged them into a familiar shape.

Then Sophie went inside. She ran
upstairs to her room. She opened her
window and looked down at the shape
she'd made.

It was a big arrow, pointing the way to Sophie's house. She hoped it was visible from the air.

chapter 9

The End?

The next morning Sophie awoke with a start. Sun was streaming in the window. She rolled over and propped herself up on her elbows. Sophie paused for a moment and crossed her fingers. What would she find under her pillow?

Then, with a dramatic flourish, she lifted it up.

The box was there. And nothing

else. Just to be sure, Sophie opened the lid. The tooth was inside.

Sophie sighed and put the pillow down again.

Well, I guess that's that, she thought. *Either I missed my chance or there is no tooth fairy.*

One thing seemed clear: The tooth fairy wasn't coming for her tooth.

Sophie got up, got dressed, and went down for breakfast. She tried not to be disappointed. But she was. She couldn't help it. Why had the

tooth fairy come for Ben's teeth, but not for hers?

Sophie felt cranky at breakfast. She snapped at Winston when he didn't pass the syrup.

"Sorry!" Winston replied. "I didn't know you needed it."

Sophie felt cranky at school, too. She told her friends what had happened: nothing.

"There must be a good reason," Ben insisted.

Sophie waved it off. "Never mind," she said. She just didn't feel like talking about it.

She was still cranky on the walk home. She spotted one of the maps they'd posted on the fir tree. She'd have to remember to take down all the maps the next day.

After dinner Sophie remembered the violets she had picked at school. She pulled them from a side pocket of her backpack. They were wilted and rumpled. But the petals were as bright as ever.

Sophie ground them into a powder. Then she mixed up a fresh tin of violet purple.

Sophie pulled out a new canvas.

She was envisioning a sunset scene. It would make excellent use of her new paint.

By the time she was done painting, Sophie was feeling much better. Painting always made her feel better.

And this sunset scene was a keeper.

"Sophie!" Winston called up the stairs. "We're going to play some board games!"

So Sophie joined them. The Mouse family always enjoyed playing board games together. And they were each good at different games, so usually Sophie and Winston didn't get *too* competitive. Between Sophie's painting and playing games with her family, it was a pretty great ending to a not-so-great day.

chapter 10

PS . . .

In the morning Sophie bounced out of bed, feeling cheerful. *I'm glad this whole tooth fairy drama is over,* she thought. *And on the bright side, I get to keep my tooth.*

Sophie looked around. Wait. Where was her tooth, anyway? The last time she saw it was . . . yesterday morning.

"Oh, right!" Sophie said out loud.

She had left the tooth box under her pillow. She had been so distracted by her disappointment that she'd forgotten to move it.

Sophie picked up her pillow.

But the box wasn't there. In its place was a single acorn.

Sophie blinked. Weird. One of the acorns from her collection must have fallen off the shelf. But then . . . how did it get *under* her pillow? That didn't make sense.

Sophie looked closer. She didn't
remember this acorn. Oh! There was
something under it—a small white
piece of paper. It blended in with
the white bedsheet, making it hard
to see.

Sophie picked up the paper. There was writing on the underside—tiny writing! Sophie had to squint to read it.

Dear Sophie,
Sorry it took me so long to bring your treat. I wanted to find the perfect acorn. I hope you like it.
Love,
T. T. F.

T. T. F.? Sophie thought. Then she gasped. The Tooth Fairy?

At the very bottom of the paper, there was even tinier writing.

PS—Thanks for the maps! It was very easy to find your house.

Sophie laughed out loud. She sup-
posed it was a good thing she'd left
the maps up, after all.

Sophie admired her newest acorn. She turned it over and over in her hand. It was perfectly round and so smooth and shiny. The color was a deep reddish-blue-black. Purple, really. A purple acorn!

Sophie didn't have anything like it. She set it down in a place of honor on her acorn shelf. It was a beautiful addition to her collection.

And it was definitely worth the wait.

The End

the adventures of
SOPHIE MOUSE

For excerpts, activities, and more about
these adorable tales & tails, visit
AdventuresofSophieMouse.com!

If you like Sophie Mouse, you'll love

the CRitteR club